DATE DUE

Cam Jansen and the Mystery of the Circus Clown

★

Also in this series

Cam Jansen and the Mystery of the Stolen Diamonds

Cam Jansen and the Mystery of the U.F.O.

Cam Jansen and the Mystery of the Dinosaur Bones

Cam Jansen and the Mystery of the Television Dog

Cam Jansen and the Mystery of the Gold Coins

Cam Jansen and the Mystery of the Babe Ruth Baseball

Cam Jansen and the Mystery of the Monster Movie

Cam Jansen and the Mystery of the Carnival Prize

Cam Jansen and the Mystery at the Monkey House

Cam Jansen and the Mystery of the Stolen Corn Popper

The JACKY WALLY CIRCUS!
PROGRAM
THE JACK WALLY CIRCUS

CAM JANSEN
and the
Mystery of the
Circus Clown

★★

DAVID A. ADLER
Illustrated by Susanna Natti

★★

The Viking Press, New York

VIKING KESTREL
Viking Penguin Inc., 40 West 23rd Street, New York, New York 10010, U.S.A.
Penguin Books Ltd, 27 Wrights Lane, London W8 5TZ (Publishing & Editorial) and
Harmondsworth, Middlesex, England (Distribution & Warehouse)
Penguin Books Australia Ltd, Ringwood, Victoria, Australia
Penguin Books Canada Limited, 2801 John Street, Markham, Ontario, Canada L3R 1B4
Penguin Books (N.Z.) Ltd, 182-190 Wairau Road, Auckland 10, New Zealand

First published in 1983 by Viking Penguin Inc.
Published simultaneously in Canada
Printed in U.S.A. by The Book Press, Brattleboro, Vermont
5 7 9 10 8 6

Library of Congress Cataloging in Publication Data
Adler, David A. Cam Jansen and the mystery of the circus clown
(The Cam Jansen adventure series; 7)
Summary: Fifth-grader Cam Jansen uses her photographic memory to help
find a pickpocket at the circus.
[1. Mystery and detective stories] [2. Circus—Fiction]
I. Natti, Susanna, ill. II. Title. III. Series: Adler, David A. Cam Jansen adventure; 7.
PZ7.A2615Cac 1983 [Fic] 82-50363 ISBN 0-670-20036-0

To my favorite boy,
Michael Seth Adler

Chapter One

Cam Jansen and her friend Eric Shelton waited while Cam's Aunt Molly bought tickets for the circus. Then they all went inside the large arena.

The lobby was noisy and crowded. Some people were rushing to their seats. Others were buying circus programs, toys, flash-lights, and whistles. Aunt Molly bought a program for Cam and a flashlight with a spinning red and blue light for Eric.

On the way to their seats a short, fat

clown bumped into Aunt Molly and then bowed to her.

Aunt Molly bowed to the clown. Then she turned to Cam and Eric and said, “I’m already having a good time.”

As they walked on, they passed another clown. He was holding a large chalkboard with the message, "Elephants are under-paid. They work for peanuts."

Aunt Molly, Cam, and Eric laughed as they read the sign. Then they walked up the stairs and through the doors into the large arena. Their seats were in the third row from the back.

"This place reminds me of the circus I saw in Montana," Aunt Molly said as she sat down. "It was in a tent. They had a bear on roller skates. I was sitting very close, and that bear kept falling off his skates. I thought he'd fall right into my lap."

While Aunt Molly spoke, Cam looked through the circus program. Eric was spinning his flashlight.

"No, I think the circus was in Mexico, or maybe it was Milwaukee. I get all those 'M' places confused."

Aunt Molly worked for an airline. She had traveled all over the world. Now she was on vacation. She was visiting Cam and her parents. It was the first time in almost ten years that she had seen Cam. The last time Aunt Molly had visited them, Cam was still a baby.

"The bears in this circus don't skate," Cam told Aunt Molly. "It says in the program that they dance and ride motorcycles."

"Oh. In the other circus it was the poodles that danced. The monkeys rode the motorcycles."

Eric put the flashlight in his pocket. Then he said to Cam, "If you give me your program, I'll give you a memory quiz."

"Just a minute," Cam said as she turned the pages of the program. As she looked at each page, she closed her eyes and said, "*Click.*"

Cam always says, "*Click,*" when she wants to remember something. "My mind is like a camera," Cam often tells people, "and cameras go '*Click.*' "

Cam's friends say that she has a mental camera. Some people call it a photographic memory. They mean that Cam remembers just about everything she sees. It's as if she had photographs stored in her brain.

Cam gave Eric the circus program and closed her eyes.

"How many elephants are in the parade?" Eric asked.

"Six. And each one wears a blue-and-gold blanket."

Eric turned the page and asked, "How many acrobats are there in the Elkans Troupe?"

"Ten, and the one in the front has red hair just like mine."

"Can you really remember all that?" Aunt Molly asked.

"Sure," Cam said. Her eyes were still closed. "And I remember that you're wearing a white blouse with pink and yellow flowers on it, and in the middle of each flower is a tiny red dot."

Cam's real name is Jennifer. But her friends started calling her "The Camera" when they heard her say, "*Click*," so often. Soon "The Camera" was shortened to "Cam."

Cam and Eric lived next door to each

other. They were in the same fifth grade class. On school nights they often did homework together.

Music started to play, and Cam opened her eyes. The lights in the arena dimmed. Eric and the other children with flashlights began spinning them. The arena was lit with hundreds of spinning blue and red lights. A spotlight was turned on, and the ringmaster walked out. The circus was about to begin.

Chapter Two

"Ladies and gentlemen and children of all ages, welcome to the Jack Wally Circus," the ringmaster called out. "Watch now as Jack Wally leads the circus parade."

The music played louder. Then an old man holding a silver cane and wearing a bright red jacket, red pants, and a white top hat walked out. Behind him were the clowns. One was juggling as he walked. Another danced in with a mop. There were clowns on stilts, one in a baby carriage, and another clown in a tiny car that he

drove backwards around the ring.

"Look," Eric said to Cam. "Here come the horses."

"And here comes the Elkans Troupe," Cam said.

There were elephants, monkeys, bears, and camels in the parade. Small dogs wearing clown hats and little skirts ran out. Circus men and women in fancy costumes smiled and waved.

"Look, here comes the circus fat lady," Cam said.

Aunt Molly laughed and said, "She looks more like a thin lady wearing lots of padding."

Just as the parade was ending, the ringmaster called out, "I direct your eyes now to the wire high above you. We proudly present the Bailor Brothers!"

"I can't look," Aunt Molly said, and covered her eyes.

Two men in bright yellow costumes

walked slowly across the high wire. They were holding long poles to help them keep their balance. When they got to the platform at the other end of the wire, the men picked up a few wooden clubs. Then they walked back onto the wire.

"What's happening now?" Aunt Molly asked.

"They're juggling," Cam said.

"And it's not scary," Eric said. "The wire isn't even shaking, and anyway, there's a safety net."

In the next acts tigers leaped through burning hoops, and elephants stood on their hind legs. Bears danced and rode motorcycles. The Elkans Troupe of acrobats built a human pyramid. The trapeze artists flew from one swing to the next, spinning and turning as they flew. Then a big cannon was rolled out.

"This is the last act before the intermission," Cam said.

The music stopped. A man dressed in silver walked out. He climbed to the top of a platform near the mouth of the cannon and waited.

"And now," the ringmaster announced, "the Jack Wally Circus is proud to present Zanger, the Human Cannonball."

Aunt Molly said, "I don't want to see this," and she closed her eyes again.

The man in silver put on a helmet. He slid down the mouth of the cannon. Some-

one lit a string at the base of the cannon. There was a loud bang and lots of smoke as the Human Cannonball flew into a net at the other end of the arena.

The people in the audience clapped. Cam, Eric, and many others stood up and cheered. Aunt Molly opened her eyes. When she saw the Human Cannonball climb out of the net, she clapped, too.

The ceiling lights went on. People hurried from their seats toward the lobby. Some children cried. Some asked for ice cream, soda, popcorn, and cotton candy.

Cam, Eric, and Aunt Molly let a small girl and her mother move by. After they passed, Aunt Molly looked on her seat and on the floor in front of her.

"What are you looking for?" Cam asked.

"My handbag. I forgot where I put it."

Cam reached under Aunt Molly's seat and took out the handbag. Aunt Molly opened it and said, "Let me give you

money so you can buy some ice cream or cotton candy."

Aunt Molly sat down. She took a scarf, a few gloves, a hairbrush, and an old woolen sock from her handbag. She put those things on her lap and looked inside her bag again. Then she said, "I had my wallet when I bought the tickets. Now I can't find it."

Cam searched through the pockets on the side of the handbag and the ones in Aunt Molly's coat. Eric looked on the floor. But the wallet was gone.

Chapter Three

Aunt Molly put the scarf, gloves, hairbrush, and woolen sock back into her handbag. Then she said, "Maybe I left the wallet at the ticket booth. Or maybe the Lost and Found has it."

"When Aunt Molly took me to the zoo," Cam told Eric, "she lost her sweater. We found one of the monkeys wearing it."

Aunt Molly said, "I do seem to lose things. Once, while I was reading in the library, I took my shoes off. I didn't remember them until I stepped in a puddle on the way home."

Aunt Molly closed her handbag. "I'm going back to the ticket booth," she said. "Do you want to come along?"

"I brought some money," Eric said. "I'd like to buy some ice cream for all of us."

Cam, Eric, and Aunt Molly walked to the large round lobby that surrounded the arena. Long lines of people were waiting to buy food and circus posters, banners and books. Other groups of people were talking and eating. Cam and Eric looked for the ice cream stand. Aunt Molly went the other way, toward the ticket booth.

As Cam and Eric walked through the lobby, they came to a crowd of laughing people. Cam stood on a bench behind the people to see what was happening.

"It's a clown," Cam told Eric.

The clown was wearing a large white jacket, and pants with red and blue stripes, and he was carrying a large brown shopping bag. The clown was short, had curly red hair, a tiny white hat, and a large red rubber nose. Two large green stars and a big smile were painted on the clown's face.

Eric climbed onto the bench next to Cam. They watched and laughed as the clown dropped a coin. The clown bent to pick up the coin and bumped into a woman. The clown bowed to apologize to the woman and then bumped into someone else. As the clown was bowing and bumping into a woman in a red dress, Cam closed her eyes and said, "*Click.*"

Cam and Eric saw Aunt Molly and got down from the bench. Aunt Molly was walking slowly. She looked around as she walked. She seemed to be lost.

Cam ran up to her and asked, "What are you looking for?"

"The Lost and Found," Aunt Molly said. "The ticket booth didn't have my wallet.

REFRESHMENTS
ICE CREAM · POPCORN ·
SODA · CANDY ·

But don't worry. I'll find it. You go and get your ice cream."

There were two lines for ice cream, one right next to the other. Cam and Eric picked what they thought was the shorter line. They were standing right behind a woman and her two children, a boy and a girl.

"The clown that bumped into Mommy didn't have a real nose," the boy told his sister.

"Yes, he did," the girl said. "I'm right, aren't I, Mommy?"

"No. I'm right," the boy said.

The woman smiled and told her children, "You're both right. The clown really has two noses. He has a clown's nose that isn't real, and right under that nose is a real one."

"What's coming next in the circus?" the boy asked.

Cam closed her eyes and said, "*Click.*"

She was looking at the picture of the circus program she had stored in her mind.

"In the second half of the circus," she told the children, "you'll see Benny's Dancing Bears. And there's Maria, a woman who is 'held in the air as she swings through the air.' You'll see Manny's Monkeys. Polly's Pink Poodles ride bicycles, and the Bailor Brothers have another high-wire act. Then the circus ends with a really big parade."

"Oh, good. Another parade," the girl said.

The line moved slowly. When the woman's turn came, the man behind the counter gave the children ice cream. Then the woman reached into her handbag for the money.

"Just a minute," the woman said. "I can't seem to find my wallet."

As she searched through her handbag, the man took the ice cream pops back from the children.

"Step aside," he said. "Let the others go."

Cam and Eric paid for their ice cream. They had started to go back to their seats when they heard a woman in the next line say, "My wallet is gone! I know I had it before, and now it's gone!"

Chapter Four

"That's the third woman who's lost her wallet," Eric said.

Cam looked at the woman in the next line. She was wearing a red dress. Cam closed her eyes and said, "*Click.*" Then she said, "*Click,*" again.

"Come on," Cam told Eric when she opened her eyes. "We have to find that clown."

Cam ran to where the clown had been just a few minutes earlier. A few people were standing there eating popcorn and cotton candy. But the clown was gone. Cam gave Eric her ice cream. She climbed onto a bench and looked around.

"There he is. I see him," Cam said, and pointed.

Cam jumped down from the bench. She and Eric tried to run through the lobby. But they couldn't get through the crowd. There were people walking slowly, holding

full cups of soda. And there were little children who kept getting into Cam and Eric's way.

"He was right here. I just saw him," Cam said when they reached an area where circus flashlights, banners, toys, and whistles were sold. Behind Cam and Eric, along the back wall of the lobby, were the rest rooms.

Eric gave one of the ice cream pops to Cam and licked some melted ice cream off his hands. Then he asked, "Why are we looking for that clown?"

"I saw him bump into that woman in the red dress. She's the same woman who was in line next to us. I said, "*Click*," when I saw it happen. I have a photograph of it stored in my mind." Cam closed her eyes. "When he bumped into her, his hand went into her handbag. I'm sure he stole her wallet. That's the clown who bumped into Aunt Molly when we came into the circus. I'll bet he bumped into the woman with the two children and took her wallet, too."

Cam opened her eyes and said, "He's probably leaving the circus right now. But he won't get far in that costume. I know just what he's wearing."

Cam said, "*Click*," and closed her eyes. "He's wearing a white jacket, red and blue striped pants, and a tiny white hat. He has red hair and floppy shoes. And he's carrying a big brown shopping bag."

While Cam was describing the clown, Eric quickly finished his ice cream. Then he looked for a place to throw the stick and wrapper. He turned and saw a clown standing just a few feet away. The clown was holding a large chalkboard.

"Look, Cam," Eric said.

Cam turned. "That's not him," she said, "but maybe he saw the Bumping Clown."

Cam and Eric quickly walked over to the clown. Cam asked him if he'd seen someone with red hair, red and blue striped

pants, and floppy shoes walk past.

The clown pointed to himself and mouthed the word, "Me."

"No, not you," Cam said. "Another clown."

The clown shook his head.

"He stole my aunt's wallet," Cam said.

The clown took a stick of chalk from his pocket and wrote on the chalkboard, "That's terrible."

"Well, a clown can't just disappear," Cam said. "We'll find him."

Cam and Eric started to walk off. Then Cam stopped. "But you *can* disappear," Cam said to the clown. "You can take off your makeup and costume. Then you'll look like everyone else. I'll bet that's what the Bumping Clown is doing—taking off his makeup."

Cam, Eric, and the clown with the chalkboard were standing near two rest rooms—a men's room and a women's room.

"I'll bet he's in there taking his makeup off right now," Cam said. She pointed to the men's room and told Eric, "You check that one. I'll check the other."

"Stop," the clown said. "One of you should check the lobby. Maybe he's still out here. Or maybe he left the arena. I'll go one way," the clown told Cam. "You go the other way."

Eric went into the men's room. Cam ran to the nearest bench. She stood on it and looked around. Since the lobby circled the arena, she could see only part of it. When she didn't see the Bumping Clown, she ran to the next group of benches.

The lights in the lobby flashed off and on. Sounds of music came from inside the arena. The second half of the circus would begin soon.

Cam got down from the bench she was standing on and ran to another one. She met Eric there.

"I didn't find him," Eric said.

"I didn't find him either," Cam said. "And now the clown with the chalkboard is gone. Let's ask the guards if they saw the Bumping Clown."

Cam and Eric went to one of the guards

standing by the doors. He was a tall man with white hair and a mustache. Cam asked him if he'd seen a clown leave.

"It's too early. The circus isn't over yet," the guard said.

"This wasn't a circus clown," Cam told him. "This clown is a pickpocket. He was

putting his hand into women's handbags and taking their wallets."

"That's some story," the guard said, and smiled. "But I didn't see any clown leave. Now you better hurry, or you'll miss the rest of the circus."

Cam and Eric walked to one of the benches. "You can go back inside," Cam told Eric, "but I want to find that clown and those wallets."

Cam and Eric sat down on the bench. They were quiet as people rushed past them to get back into the arena. Then Eric said, "Maybe what you told that guard was wrong. Maybe that pickpocket *is* one of the circus clowns. Maybe he went back inside and he'll be in the second half of the circus."

Cam said, "That's easy to find out. All the clowns' pictures are in the program." Then she closed her eyes and said, "*Click.*"

Chapter Five

"Oh, there you are. I lose so many things I was afraid that I'd lost you," Aunt Molly said as she walked toward the bench. "Let's hurry back inside."

Cam opened her eyes and asked, "Did you find your wallet?"

"No."

"Cam knows who took it," Eric said. "It was one of the clowns, the one who bumped into you after you bought the tickets."

Cam closed her eyes and said, "*Click.*"

Eric whispered to Aunt Molly, "She's looking at the pictures she has in her head of all the clowns in the circus program."

"Can she really do that?" Aunt Molly asked.

Cam said, "*Click*," again.

Eric whispered, "Now she's looking at another page in the program."

"Amazing."

Cam opened her eyes and said, "He's not one of the circus clowns."

"Well, he's not a clown, I can tell you that," Aunt Molly said as she sat down. "He's just a man dressed as a clown. Let me tell you something. If you see a flower in a garden, it's beautiful. If you see it in the middle of a green lawn, it's a weed."

"Aunt Molly, we don't have time now to talk about flowers," Cam said.

"I'm not talking about flowers. I'm talking about people. I've been to a great many places. In Scotland a man wearing a kilt wouldn't surprise me. A kilt is like a skirt, you know. But in Chicago I would turn to look at him."

"What do you mean?"

"I mean that if the clown is smart, he'll just take off his makeup. That way he doesn't even have to hide at all. He'll look like everyone else."

"But I checked the men's room," Eric said. "And I didn't see anyone wearing funny clown shoes or a costume or standing in front of the mirror taking off makeup."

Aunt Molly pointed to a man leaving the circus. He was carrying a large brown shopping bag. "Did you see him?" she asked.

"Let's go," Cam said, and she ran toward the man. Eric followed her.

"Why did you do it? Why did you take Aunt Molly's wallet?" Cam yelled as she ran.

The man stopped.

"We know who you are," Eric said. "You're the Bumping Clown. And you've got your costume and Aunt Molly's wallet in that bag."

"I'm not a clown. I sell hot dogs."

The man reached into the bag and took out a red and white striped apron and a hat. The sign on the hat said, "Hot Dogs."

Cam and Eric apologized to the man. Then, as they were walking back to Aunt Molly, two other men walked toward them. They were both carrying shopping bags.

"Do you sell hot dogs?" Cam asked one of them.

"No, cotton candy."

"And I sell popcorn."

Cam and Eric went back to the bench. Cam sat down. Then she said, "*Click*," and closed her eyes.

"That clown had a lot of makeup on," Cam said with her eyes closed. "It would take a long time for him to take off all that makeup and his costume."

"Well, he didn't take it off in the rest room," Eric said. "Maybe he's hiding somewhere."

"If what Aunt Molly said about flowers and weeds and kilts is true, that clown doesn't have to hide. He could be inside running around with the other clowns. But if he found someplace to take off his makeup, he's probably sitting and watching the circus. Come on," Cam said as she got up from her seat. "We have to find him now. When the circus ends, and everyone leaves he'll get lost in the crowd."

Chapter Six

Cam ran through the lobby and up the stairs to the doors that led into the arena. Eric followed her.

"Wait for me," Aunt Molly called.

Cam and Eric waited. When Aunt Molly reached the top of the steps, Cam said, "First look at the clowns. If you don't see him there, look around at all the people watching the circus."

Cam was about to open the door to the arena when Aunt Molly told her to wait again.

"If the clown took off his makeup, how will we find him?" Aunt Molly asked.

"You're right," Cam said as she turned away from the door. Then she closed her eyes and said, "*Click.*" She looked at the picture of the clown she had stored in her mind.

"It's hard to tell what he looks like behind all that makeup. He may have curly red hair, or it may have been a wig. But I do know that he's short and he was carrying a shopping bag."

Cam opened her eyes. Then Eric opened the door and they walked inside. In the center of the arena Manny's Monkeys were skating in a circle. As the monkeys skated faster, the circle got bigger.

The monkeys left the circus ring, and the clowns came out. Cam looked at each of them. She didn't see the Bumping Clown.

Cam looked at the large crowd watching the circus. She saw only the backs of the people sitting near her. The people on the other side of the arena were just dots of color.

Cam saw someone with curly red hair. There was something on his lap that looked like a shopping bag. Cam ran down the aisle. But when she got closer, Cam saw that it was a woman. A little boy was sitting on her lap.

While Cam, Eric, and Aunt Molly looked around at the crowd, Polly's Pink Poodles rode bicycles around the center of the arena. Then the ringmaster called out, "I direct your eyes to the high wire for another look at the amazing Bailor Brothers."

The two brothers walked slowly across the wire. They took turns riding a bicycle on the wire. Then one of the brothers sat on a chair balanced on the high wire.

Restless children were moving around in their seats. Some people were standing to get a better look at the Bailor Brothers. Cam looked up. One of the Bailors was standing on the high wire. His brother was balanced on his shoulders. The crowd stood and cheered as the Bailors walked carefully across the wire to the platform and down the ladder.

Jack Wally walked out, and the parade began. The clowns and acrobats marched out. The horses and elephants came next. People were clapping and cheering.

Cam waved to Eric and Aunt Molly. She pointed toward the lobby and signaled to them to meet her there.

People were beginning to leave their seats. Children who didn't want the circus to end were crying. Music played. Four horses came out pulling a red, white, and blue wagon. There was a loud cheer for the Bailor Brothers. They were in the last wagon of the parade.

The lights in the arena were turned on. Cam stood still and watched as people walked past her. She saw a few short men walk by, but she had no way of knowing if one of them was the Bumping Clown. Then Cam saw a thin young man standing just ahead of her. The man was carrying a large shopping bag and a chalkboard. There was some yellow and green makeup still on his face.

That's the clown who helped us before, Cam said to herself. "Hi," she called to him and waved.

The clown didn't wave back. He pulled at the sleeve of the woman standing next to him. Cam saw a little green make-up on her face, too.

The two of them quickly pushed through the crowd toward the doors. Cam tried to catch up with them. When she got to the doors, she saw they were already downstairs, running through the lobby.

Chapter Seven

Cam ran down the steps to the lobby. Eric and Aunt Molly were waiting for her.

"I saw the clown with the chalkboard, the one who helped us before," Cam said. "He was with a short woman, and they're both carrying shopping bags. I think she's the pickpocket."

Cam ran through the doors and onto the sidewalk. Eric and Aunt Molly followed her. It was raining hard outside. Some people had umbrellas. Others covered their heads with magazines and newspapers as they ran to their cars. Cam, Eric, and Aunt Molly looked for the couple.

"Is that them?" Eric asked. He pointed to a man and woman walking quickly toward the parking lot.

"Yes."

"You get the guard," Aunt Molly said as she took a scarf from her handbag. "I'll stall them."

Eric ran back to the arena. Aunt Molly walked quickly toward the couple. Cam followed her.

"Excuse me," Aunt Molly said to them, "but do you have the time?"

"It's four-thirty," the woman called out over the sound of the pouring rain.

Aunt Molly stood in front of the woman as the man walked ahead. "You know it's not four-thirty in London," Aunt Molly said. "It's later there. I travel a lot and I never really know what time it is. That's why I ask people."

"Come on," the man called.

"Please, I'm getting all wet," the woman said. "And I'm in a hurry."

While they were talking, Cam sneaked behind the woman and looked in the woman's bag. She saw a red wig, a white jacket, and pants with red and blue stripes. Cam was standing behind the woman. She pointed to her and nodded her head so that Aunt Molly would know they had found the Bumping Clown.

"People over here always seem to be in a hurry," Aunt Molly said. "It's not like that all over, you know."

The woman started to push past Aunt Molly. The man was coming to help. Just then two of the guards ran up.

"You, over there. Stop!"

The woman started to run off, but she slipped on the wet street and fell. The man ran to his car. As he was opening the door, the guards caught up with him. They led him back to where the woman was sitting on the wet street. The guards helped her up and led them both back to the arena. Cam, Eric, and Aunt Molly walked behind them.

They all went into an office behind the

ticket booth. The woman sat down with the shopping bag on her lap. The man stood next to her. One of the guards called the police.

The woman's dress was soaking wet. The paper shopping bag she was holding was wet too. Aunt Molly took a handkerchief from her handbag and wiped the rain from her face. Then she gave the handkerchief to Cam.

"Why are you holding us here?" the man asked. "We did nothing wrong."

"And look at me. I'm all wet," the woman said.

"You stole my wallet. That's why we stopped you," Aunt Molly said.

"And you took other people's wallets, too," Cam said. "And I'll bet they're all in those bags you're holding."

"I didn't take anything," the man said.

"Neither did I. Everything in this bag is mine," the woman said, and lifted her bag.

As she lifted it, a big hole ripped through the bottom of the wet bag. Clown shoes, a jacket, pants, a small white hat, a red wig, and several wallets fell out.

Aunt Molly picked up one of the wallets. She opened it and took out a credit card. She showed the card to one of the guards and said, "This is mine."

Chapter Eight

Jack Wally walked into the office. He was still wearing his bright red suit and carrying his top hat. He wrote a list of all the names and telephone numbers of the people whose wallets were stolen. He said that he would call the people and tell them that their wallets had been found.

Then the police came. "So it's you two again," one of them said. "The last time we caught you, you were dressed as train conductors. One of you picked pockets while the other one looked out for the real conductor."

"That's what they did this time," Cam said. "She picked the pockets while he made sure that they weren't caught. We didn't find them right away because with her clown's costume on, we thought the Bumping Clown was a man. We looked for her in the lobby and in the men's room. It was the clown with the chalkboard who stopped me from looking in the women's room. The Bumping Clown was probably in there the whole time taking off her makeup."

"And the other one probably took his makeup off while we were talking to the guard," Eric said.

The police looked through the man's shopping bag. They found his clown costume and a few wallets in there.

"I see you were more than just a lookout this time," one of the police officers said. "Well, come with us."

The woman picked up her clown costume from the floor. She dropped the wig on her head, and the police led her and her partner away.

"I'm really glad you caught them," Jack Wally told Cam, Eric, and Aunt Molly. "First I want to give you passes to see the

circus again. One of the guards told me that you missed most of the second half."

Jack Wally reached into his hat and took out a few slips of paper. "Now what are your names?"

"I'm Jennifer Jansen," Cam said.

"I'm Eric Shelton."

"And I'm Molly Jansen."

Jack Wally wrote their names on the circus passes. Then he asked, "Do you have sisters or brothers you'd like to bring to the circus?"

"I do," Eric said. "I have twin sisters, Donna and Diane, and a baby brother, Howie."

Jack Wally took three more passes from his hat. He wrote on the passes and gave them to Eric. Then he said, "Come on. I'll get you some circus programs and flashlights. Then we'll meet the Bailor Brothers."

Cam, Eric, and Aunt Molly followed Jack Wally to his office. As they walked there,

Cam and Eric thanked Aunt Molly for taking them to the circus. They said they had had a good time. "And the best part," Eric said, "is that we're going to meet the Bailor Brothers."

Jack Wally gave them the programs and flashlights. Then they followed him to a small dressing room. One of the Bailors was sitting with his feet up on the dressing table. The other one had his feet soaking in a bucket of hot, soapy water.

"I'd like you to meet some heroes," Jack Wally said to the Bailor Brothers. "Maybe you can autograph their programs."

The two brothers signed the programs. Then the one with his feet in the bucket of water asked, "What did you do to become heroes?"

"Well," Aunt Molly said, "my niece Jennifer and her friend Eric caught two clowns who were pickpockets. Jennifer has an amazing memory. She has a head full of

PROGRAM
THE JACK WOLLY CIRCUS

pictures and that's how she remembers things and finds people. And do you know how Jennifer takes pictures and looks at them? She just closes her eyes and says, 'Clock.' "

"Cam doesn't say, 'Clock,' " Eric said.

"Cluck?"

"No."

"Clack?"

Cam laughed and said, "No. I make the same sound a real camera makes."

Cam looked at Eric, Aunt Molly, the Bailor Brothers, and Jack Wally. "Smile," she said. "I'm taking your picture." Then Cam closed her eyes and said, "*Click.*"